Runny Honey

by Jane Clarke

Illustrated by Tomislav Zlatic

W
FRANKLIN WATTS
LONDON•SYDNEY

Jane Clarke

"I love eating runny honey on buttered toast, but I would never stick my nose in the jar!"

Tomislav Zlatic

"I started liking honey when I was very young. It's funny, but when you start to mess with it, you just can't get rid of it. It's so sticky!"

Runny honey!
Yummy! Yummy!

5

Runny honey
on Bear's paws.

6

7

Runny honey
in Bear's jaws.

Runny honey in Bear's tummy.

Runny honey
on Bear's nose.

Runny honey
on Bear's toes.

13

Runny honey
everywhere!
On the table,
on the chair ...

on the walls ...

on the floor ...

on the window ...

and on the door.

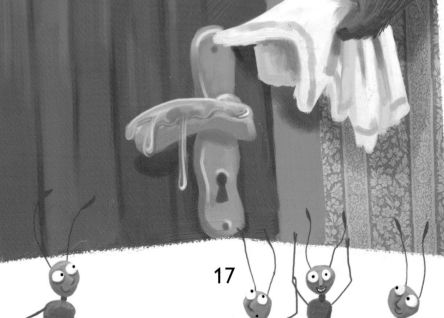

Runny honey
in Bear's hair.

18

Runny honey everywhere!

Runny honey
in Bear's pants.

Run, Bear, run!
Here come the ...

21

... ANTS!

22

Notes for adults

TADPOLES are structured to provide support for newly independent readers. The stories may also be used by adults for sharing with young children.

Starting to read alone can be daunting. **TADPOLES** help by providing visual support and repeating words and phrases. These books will both develop confidence and encourage reading and rereading for pleasure.

If you are reading this book with a child, here are a few suggestions:

1. Make reading fun! Choose a time to read when you and the child are relaxed and have time to share the story.

2. Talk about the story before you start reading. Look at the cover and the blurb. What might the story be about? Why might the child like it?

3. Encourage the child to reread the story, and to retell the story in their own words, using the illustrations to remind them what has happened.

4. Discuss the story and see if the child can relate it to their own experience, or perhaps compare it to another story they know.

5. Give praise! Remember that small mistakes need not always be corrected.

If you enjoyed this book,
why not try another TADPOLES story?

Sammy's Secret
978 0 7496 6890 7

Mop Top
978 0 7946 6895 2

Stroppy Poppy
978 0 7496 6893 8

Charlie and the Castle
978 0 7496 6896 9

I'm Taller Than You!
978 0 7496 6894 5

Over the Moon!
978 0 7496 6897 6

Leo's New Pet
978 0 7496 6891 4

My Sister is a Witch!
978 0 7496 6898 3